D0181571

THIRD-GRADE
DETECTIVES #1

The Clue of the
Left-Handed
Envelope

THIRD-GRADE
DETECTIVES #2

The Puzzle of the
Pretty Pink
Handkerchief

This book is dedicated to the wonderful students

in Mrs. Schlueter's third-grade class at

Lincoln Elementary School in Norman, Oklahoma.

You're great! Thanks for all your help.

First Aladdin Paperbacks edition June 2004

Third-Grade Detectives #1: The Clue of the Left-Handed Envelope
text copyright © 2000 by George E. Stanley
Third-Grade Detectives #1: The Clue of the Left-Handed Envelope
illustrations copyright © 2000 by Salvatore Murdocca
Third-Grade Detectives #2: The Puzzle of the Pretty Pink Handkerchief
text copyright © 2000 by George E. Stanley
Third-Grade Detectives #2: The Puzzle of the Pretty Pink Handkerchief
illustrations copyright © 2000 by Salvatore Murdocca

ALADDIN PAPERBACKS
An imprint of Simon & Schuster Children's Publishing Division
1230 Avenue of the Americas
New York, NY 10020

Designed by Steve Scott
The text for this book was set in 14-point Lino Letter.
Printed in the United States of America
16 18 20 19 17

Library of Congress Control Number 98-10579 *(The Clue of the Left-Handed Envelope)*
Library of Congress Control Number 98-10576 *(The Puzzle of the Pretty Pink Handkerchief)*
ISBN 978-0-689-87106-1
These titles were previously published individually.

0817 OFF

THIRD-GRADE DETECTIVES #1

The Clue of the
Left-Handed Envelope

THIRD-GRADE DETECTIVES #2

The Puzzle of the
Pretty Pink Handkerchief

George E. Stanley

illustrated by
Salvatore Murdocca

Aladdin Paperbacks
New York London Toronto Sydney

THIRD-GRADE DETECTIVES #1

The Clue of the
Left-Handed
Envelope

Chapter One

It was the first day of the third grade, and Noelle Trocoderro was late.

She ran down the sidewalk outside the school building.

All summer long, Noelle had been looking forward to starting school again.

Mrs. Trumble would be her teacher this year.

Everyone loved Mrs. Trumble.

She was the nicest teacher in the whole school.

Finally, Noelle reached Mrs. Trumble's third-grade classroom.

She stopped at the door.

There was a *man* writing on the chalkboard.

Something's wrong here, Noelle thought.

She looked around.

Her friend Todd Sloan was waving to her.

Todd lived across the street from Noelle.

They did a lot of things together.

Noelle thought Todd was more interesting than most of the girls in her class.

She hurried over and sat down in the empty seat next to him.

"Who's that man?" Noelle whispered.

"Mr. Merlin," Todd replied. "He's our new teacher."

"What happened to Mrs. Trumble?" Noelle asked.

"She moved," Todd said. He leaned closer to Noelle. "Amber Lee Johnson said Mr. Merlin used to be a spy."

Noelle blinked. "How did she find that out?"

Todd shrugged.

Noelle looked at Mr. Merlin again.

She liked spy shows on television.

Maybe she wouldn't miss Mrs. Trumble after all.

Mr. Merlin stopped writing on the chalk-board.

He turned around and faced the class.

"Good morning, class. I'm Mr. Merlin. I'm your new teacher," he said. "I used to be a spy."

Leon Dennis raised his hand. "What did you do when you were a spy?"

"I caught lots and lots of other spies," Mr. Merlin said. "I used lots and lots of secret codes, too."

Todd leaned over to Noelle. "Amber Lee said he did those things in *foreign countries*," he whispered.

Noelle looked at him. "Really?" she whispered back.

Todd nodded.

"Going to school is like solving a mystery," Mr. Merlin continued. "We're going to solve a lot of mysteries this year."

"What kinds of mysteries?" Amber Lee asked.

"All kinds," Mr. Merlin said.

He looked around the classroom.

"Does anyone here have a mystery we can start with?" he asked.

Noelle sighed.

She wished she had a mystery so she could impress Mr. Merlin.

"I have a mystery," Amber Lee said.

"What's your mystery?" Mr. Merlin asked.

Amber Lee stood up.

She waved an envelope at everyone.

"This came for me in the mail yesterday," she said. "I want to know who sent it."

"What does it say?" Mr. Merlin asked.

Amber Lee took a letter out of the envelope and started reading.

"'Dear Amber Lee, you are the smartest girl in the world.' It's signed: 'An Admirer.'"

She looked at Mr. Merlin.

"If I knew who sent it," she said, "I could say thank you."

Mr. Merlin smiled.

Noelle rolled her eyes at Todd.

"That's not a mystery," she whispered. "Amber Lee probably sent that letter to herself."

Todd nodded his agreement.

"Okay," Mr. Merlin said. "We'll solve the mystery of who wrote Amber Lee the letter."

He turned around.

He started writing on the chalkboard.

He wrote:

E E N
P X V
O L E

"But first you all have to solve a secret code," he said.

"Why do we have to do that?" Leon asked. "Why can't we just solve the mystery?"

"Secret codes are fun," Mr. Merlin said. "They also help you learn to think better."

"I already know how to think," Leon said. "I don't like to do it too much."

"Well, you'll want to think about this," Mr. Merlin said. "There's a clue in it that will tell you where to start so you can solve the mystery."

Chapter Two

"That looks easy," Amber Lee said.

Mr. Merlin smiled.

Amber Lee is such a show-off! Noelle thought.

She looked around the room.

Everyone was busy trying to solve the secret code.

Noelle raised her hand.

She had to wave it around several minutes before Mr. Merlin saw it.

"Yes?" Mr. Merlin said.

"I think it looks easy, too," Noelle said.

Mr. Merlin smiled again.

Amber Lee gave Noelle a dirty look.

"I don't think it looks easy," Todd whispered.

Noelle didn't think it looked easy, either, but

she wasn't going to admit that to anyone.

Mr. Merlin let them work on the secret code for fifteen minutes.

When the time was up, nobody had solved it.

Mr. Merlin stood up.

"If you're a spy, you may have to solve secret codes without any help," he said.

"But sometimes you have a codebook to use.

"The codebook has rules to follow.

"I'll give you three rules for this secret code."

Great! Noelle thought. If she had the rules, she was sure she could solve the secret code.

Then she could solve the mystery.

Mr. Merlin wrote the rules on the chalkboard.

He wrote them next to the secret code:

1. The middle of the clock is X.
2. You need to start at noon.
3. You should follow the hands.

Noelle studied the rules carefully.

The middle of the clock is X.

What clock was he talking about? she wondered.

She saw an *X*, but she didn't see a clock.

You need to start at noon.

Did that mean they had to wait until noon?

No! Mr. Merlin had told them to work on it now.

You should follow the hands.

What hands? Noelle wondered. She didn't see any hands, either.

She sighed.

She rested her chin in her hands.

From where she was sitting, she could see the big clock on the wall of the classroom.

She always liked to watch the big red second hand as it raced around the numbers.

It made her think that. . . .

She stopped.

That's it! she thought.

She raised her hand.

"I can solve it, Mr. Merlin!" she said excitedly.

Chapter Three

Amber Lee stood up. "She can't solve my mystery!" she cried.

"Amber Lee!" Mr. Merlin said. "Please sit down!"

He took a deep breath.

"Remember that you're the one who asked the class to solve your mystery," he said.

Amber Lee sat down.

She rolled her eyes at the ceiling.

"Oh, okay," she said.

Mr. Merlin looked at Noelle. "You may tell us what you think the secret code says."

Noelle walked to the front of the room.

She smiled at everyone.

She even smiled at Amber Lee.

She tried to make it a nice smile.

Amber Lee pretended to read a book.

"This secret code was very hard," Noelle said.

"I thought and thought and thought and thought and thought and thought and thought and thought and thought and—"

"Okay, Noelle. We get the picture," Mr. Merlin said. "Please continue."

"Finally, when I saw the big red second hand on the clock," Noelle continued, "I knew how to do it.

"You pretend that *X* is the middle of a real clock.

"If you start at noon, that means you start at twelve o'clock.

"On a real clock, twelve would be the middle *E* on the top line.

"If you follow the hands, then you write the letters the way the hands on a clock would go:
E N V E L O P E

"The secret code clue is *envelope!*"

"Excellent!" Mr. Merlin said.

He held up the envelope that Amber Lee's letter had come in.

"To solve this mystery, you need to start with

the envelope," Mr. Merlin said.

"What's so special about the envelope?" Amber Lee asked. "It just looks like a plain old envelope to me."

Mr. Merlin turned around.

He started writing on the chalkboard again. He wrote:

A S B
L X A
I V A

"Here's a new secret code clue," he said. "It'll tell you something you need to know about the envelope."

"*Sbaavila!*" Amber Lee cried.

The class laughed.

Mr. Merlin smiled.

"Good try, Amber Lee," he said. "But this is a different secret code."

Noelle had started to say *sbaavila,* too.

She was glad she hadn't.

But now she didn't know what this new secret code clue meant, either.

"Here are some new rules," Mr. Merlin said.

"The middle of the clock is X.

"You need to start at noon.

"You should go the other way."

Noelle raised her hand.

"Salivaab!" Amber Lee shouted.

"Excellent!" Mr. Merlin said.

Noelle knew it, too.

She wished she had just shouted it out like Amber Lee had.

"But leave off the *ab* at the end, Amber Lee. Those are just the first two letters of the alphabet," Mr. Merlin said. "They're only used to fill up the square."

"Saliva?" Misty Goforth said. "What's that?"

"Spit!" Todd said. "It's spit!"

"Oh, yuck!" Amber Lee said.

Noelle frowned. *What did spit have to do with solving this mystery?* she wondered.

Chapter Four

Noelle had just started to ask Mr. Merlin that question when a woman knocked on the door of the classroom.

Mr. Merlin looked up.

"Come in, Dr. Smiley!" he said.

Dr. Smiley came into the classroom.

"Class, Dr. Smiley is a scientist. She works for the police," Mr. Merlin said. "I asked her to tell you all about what she does."

Dr. Smiley smiled at the class.

Then she told them how she used science to solve crimes.

When she finished, she said, "I'll even show you how I do it one of these days."

The class applauded

Todd looked over at Noelle.

"I didn't know policemen were so pretty," he whispered.

"She's not a police*man*," Noelle said. "She's a police*woman*."

"Actually, she's a police *scientist*," Todd said.

Noelle thought Dr. Smiley was pretty, too.

"I wonder if Dr. Smiley and Mr. Merlin are a couple?" she whispered. "She keeps smiling at him. Only couples smile at each other that way."

"I'll ask," Todd whispered.

He raised his hand.

"No, Todd! You don't ask people things like that!" Noelle whispered. "I'll find out some other way."

She looked over at Amber Lee.

Noelle was sure Amber Lee would know.

Amber Lee seemed to know everything about everybody.

Noelle would have to ask her.

Amber Lee liked it when people asked her questions.

✉   ✉   ✉

The rest of the day, they did their schoolwork.

When the final bell rang, Noelle and Todd left the classroom together.

"I asked Amber Lee if Mr. Merlin and Dr. Smiley were a couple," Noelle said.

"What'd she say?" Todd asked.

"She didn't say anything," Noelle said. "She just grinned."

"She knows," Todd said. "I know she knows."

"You have to come to my house," Noelle said. "We have to solve this mystery before Amber Lee does."

"Why are you so worried about this mystery?" Todd asked. "I'm getting bored with it."

Noelle looked at him. "You've always liked mysteries before. Why don't you like this one?"

"I don't care who sent Amber Lee that stupid letter," Todd said.

"But I need your help, Todd. If Amber Lee solves the mystery first, people really will think she's the smartest girl in the world. She'll never let me forget it, either."

"Oh, all right," Todd said.

When they got to Noelle's house, Todd called his mother to tell her where he was.

Then he and Noelle went to Noelle's room.

"Okay," Todd said. "What do we do first?"

"We think about envelopes and spit," Noelle said. "Those are the two clues that Mr. Merlin gave us."

So they thought about envelopes and spit for several minutes.

Then suddenly Noelle jumped up.

"Of course!" she shouted. "Come on!"

She started out of her room.

Todd was right behind her.

They went downstairs to the den.

Noelle opened the bottom drawer of a big desk.

She took out a big box of envelopes.

"Now we can solve this mystery," she said.

"How?" Todd asked.

"You use spit to lick envelopes," Noelle said. "So we'll lick all of these envelopes until we figure out what the mystery is."

"That is so dumb, Noelle," Todd said.

"No, it's not. My dad does it all the time," Noelle said. "It's called *trial and error*."

"What does that mean?" Todd asked.

"It means you have to keep making mistakes over and over until you get it right," Noelle said.

They went back upstairs to Noelle's room.

Noelle handed Todd an envelope.

"You start," she said.

Todd stuck out his tongue.

He licked the flap.

"Ugh!" he said. "That glue tastes awful!"

He looked at Noelle.

"Did you notice anything when I licked it?" he asked.

Noelle sighed. "Nothing. That must have been an error." She picked up an envelope. "Watch me."

"Okay," Todd said.

Noelle licked the flap of her envelope.

Todd was right, she thought.

The glue tasted awful.

"What happened when I licked the flap?" Noelle asked.

"Nothing," Todd said. "I guess it's another error."

"You didn't see anything that would help

us solve the mystery?" Noelle said.

Todd shook his head. "No."

"We're missing something here," Noelle said.

"We have spit.

"We have envelopes.

"Those are the two things Mr. Merlin said we needed to solve the mystery."

She sighed.

"I guess we'll just have to keep licking these envelope flaps and watching each other until we figure something out."

They took turns watching each other lick envelope flaps.

Finally, there were no more envelope flaps to lick.

"I don't have any more spit in my mouth, anyway," Todd said.

"Me, either," Noelle said.

She looked down at the floor.

It was covered with envelopes.

They were all stuck together.

Noelle just hoped her parents weren't planning to write any letters soon.

"Now what?" Todd said.

"Maybe Mr. Merlin will give us some more clues tomorrow," Noelle said. "I just hope that Amber Lee hasn't already solved the mystery."

Chapter Five

Noelle hurried down the sidewalk toward Mr. Merlin's classroom.

When she reached the door, she stopped.

"Please don't let Amber Lee have solved the mystery," she whispered.

She held her breath.

Then she slowly went inside.

She looked over at Amber Lee.

She let out her breath.

She knew she could relax now.

Amber Lee didn't look very happy.

In fact, Amber Lee looked really mad.

Noelle was sure that meant Amber Lee still didn't know who had sent her the letter.

Suddenly, someone touched Noelle's shoulder.

She whirled around.

It was Leon.

He was holding a glass jar.

"Spit in this jar," Leon said.

"*What?*" Noelle cried.

"Spit in this jar," Leon repeated.

"Why?" Noelle demanded.

"I need some of your spit," Leon said.

"No!" Noelle said.

She went on into the classroom.

Leon followed her.

"Spit in this jar, Noelle!" Leon whispered. "I have to have some of your spit!"

Noelle took her seat next to Todd.

She ignored Leon.

Finally, he walked away and took his seat.

"What's going on?" Noelle whispered to Todd. "Why did Leon want me to spit in that jar?"

"Amber Lee is having some of her friends collect spit for her," Todd whispered. "She said that's what police do. She saw it on television last night."

Noelle wondered if she should be collecting spit, too.

She decided she just couldn't go around

asking people to spit into a glass jar.

She looked around.

Several people in the class were holding glass jars.

Noelle could see the jars had something in the bottom of them.

Spit!

For a moment, she thought she was going to be sick.

Then the bell rang.

And Mr. Merlin started class.

"Did anybody solve the mystery?" he asked.

"I've almost solved it," Amber Lee said. "My friends and I are collecting spit from everyone."

Mr. Merlin blinked. "Would you care to explain that, Amber Lee?" he said.

Amber Lee stood up.

"It's what police do," she said. "I saw it on television last night."

"Well, it is true that police detectives often collect saliva samples from suspects," Mr. Merlin said, "but you have to be very careful about doing that because of diseases."

"Ugh!" Amber Lee's friends cried.

They all dropped their glass jars.

The glass jars fell to the floor.

Now, there was spit and glass all over the place.

Several people screamed.

They put their feet up on their desks.

Noelle saw Mr. Merlin take a deep breath and let it out.

But he didn't get angry.

Instead, he sent Leon to get the janitor.

While the janitor was mopping up the floor, everyone copied the day's spelling words off the chalkboard.

When the janitor finished, Mr. Merlin said, "Now, then. Back to our mystery. What are the rest of you doing?"

Noelle raised her hand.

"Yes?" Mr. Merlin said.

"Todd and I licked all of the envelopes at our house last night," she said. "We watched each other. But we didn't notice anything unusual."

"Well, you and Todd are on the right track, Noelle," Mr. Merlin said.

Noelle smiled.

Amber Lee frowned.

"I'll give you another clue," Mr. Merlin said. "To solve this mystery, you really do need to start with saliva, but it's the saliva on the flap of Amber Lee's envelope."

Amber Lee gasped.

"Let's do an experiment," Mr. Merlin said. "I have envelopes for everyone."

He passed out the envelopes.

"Hold them up in front of you," Mr. Merlin continued.

All the kids in the class held up the envelopes in front of them.

"On three, I want everyone to lick the flaps," Mr. Merlin said. "Ready? One, two, *three!*"

Noelle licked the flap of her envelope.

So did the rest of the class.

They made loud, slurping noises.

Everyone laughed.

"Now, then, class, I'm going to lick the flap of another envelope," Mr. Merlin said.

Mr. Merlin turned his back to the class.

"Watch me carefully," he said.

He held up another envelope.

He licked the flap.

He turned back around to face the class.

"Which side of the flap did I start on?" he asked.

No one said anything.

It's a trick question, Noelle thought. She hadn't paid any attention to that.

She closed her eyes.

She tried to remember which side of the envelope flap Mr. Merlin had started on.

She then tried to remember which side of the envelope flap she had started on.

She thought she and Mr. Merlin had both started on the same side.

The left.

Noelle opened her eyes.

"The left?" she shouted.

"Correct!" Mr. Merlin said. "Now I'm going to give you another clue," he added. "I'm right-handed."

That's not much of a clue, Noelle thought.

Mr. Merlin looked at the class. "So what question would a good police detective ask next?" he said.

Chapter Six

Several people raised their hands.

Noelle couldn't believe it.

She didn't know the answer yet.

She held her breath.

"Put your hands down. I want everyone to think about it for a while. That's what a good police detective would do," Mr. Merlin said. "I'll ask you again after we've finished reading in our reader."

Noelle let out her breath.

She hoped Mr. Merlin didn't call on her to read.

She had to use that time to think up a question that a good police detective would ask next.

"Open your readers to page ten," Mr. Merlin said.

He looked around the class.

"Who wants to read first?" he asked.

Noelle ducked her head.

She pretended she was still trying to find page ten.

"I do," Amber Lee said.

Noelle looked up.

Oh, no! she thought.

Amber Lee must already know the next question a good police detective would ask.

Why would she waste her time reading if she didn't?

She'd be thinking about the question instead.

Of course, Noelle knew that Amber Lee liked to show off.

Amber Lee thought she was the best reader in the class.

Well, just let Amber Lee show off! Noelle decided.

When reading was over, Noelle would know the question, too!

Amber Lee started reading.

Noelle started thinking.

She thought about everything that Mr. Merlin had told them.

She thought about envelopes.

She thought about spit.

She thought about how Mr. Merlin had licked his flap from left to right.

She thought about how she had done the same thing.

She took a deep breath and then let it out.

Now what? she wondered.

She looked over at Todd.

Todd was following along in the reader as Amber Lee read.

Sometimes Noelle was so disappointed in Todd.

He should be thinking about the question, too.

Noelle sighed.

Had Todd licked his envelope flap from left to right? she wondered.

Suddenly, Noelle had an idea.

She poked Todd in the ribs.

Todd looked up.

"Show me how you licked your flap," Noelle whispered.

Todd rolled his eyes.

But he held up a *pretend* envelope.

He licked the flap.

Noelle felt her heart skip a beat.

"Do it again!" she whispered.

"No talking, please!" Mr. Merlin said.

Noelle turned.

Mr. Merlin was staring at her.

She pretended to cough.

Then she pretended to look at her reader.

After a few minutes, Amber Lee stopped reading.

Leon began reading.

Noelle was glad.

Mr. Merlin had to help him with every other word.

He would be too busy pronouncing words for Leon to notice what Noelle was doing.

Noelle gave Todd another poke.

"Lick your flap again," she whispered.

Todd rolled his eyes.

But he pretended to lick another envelope flap.

"That's it!" Noelle whispered. "I know what the question is!"

Chapter Seven

"Well, that's enough reading for today," Mr. Merlin finally said.

The class put away their readers.

Noelle looked over at Amber Lee.

Amber Lee still had a smile on her face.

Somehow, Noelle had to make sure Amber Lee wasn't the first one to tell Mr. Merlin what the question was.

She decided to take a chance.

"I know the question, Mr. Merlin," Noelle said. "Do you want me to tell the class?"

Amber Lee jerked her head around to look at Noelle.

Then she jumped out of her seat.

Her desk almost fell over.

"I know the question, too, Mr. Merlin," she

shouted. "It's 'Did a boy or a girl lick the flap of the envelope?'"

Noelle couldn't believe that Amber Lee had beaten her.

She looked over at Mr. Merlin.

Oh, please don't make that the question! she pleaded silently.

"Well, that's a good question, Amber Lee," Mr. Merlin said, "but I'm afraid that's not what a police detective would ask next."

He turned to Noelle.

"What do you think the question is?" he asked.

Noelle took a deep breath.

Here goes, she thought.

"I think the question is, 'Which side did the person start on when he licked the envelope flap?'"

"That's exactly right!" Mr. Merlin said.

Amber Lee started crying.

"What's wrong, Amber Lee?" Mr. Merlin asked.

"That's what I was going to say next," Amber Lee sobbed. "You didn't give me a chance to finish."

"Oh, I'm sorry," Mr. Merlin said. "Well, next time please remind me to give you more time to answer the question."

Amber Lee stopped crying.

"How can you find out which side the person started on?" Todd asked.

"You unseal the envelope flap scientifically," Mr. Merlin explained.

"Then you put special chemicals on it.

"I asked Dr. Smiley to test Amber Lee's envelope.

"The flap had more saliva on the right-hand side.

"It decreased across the arc to the left-hand side.

"That means whoever licked the envelope flap probably started on the right-hand side and licked to the left-hand side."

Mr. Merlin looked around the room.

"Think about it carefully," he said. "Which hand does this person probably use?"

Amber Lee raised her hand.

"He probably uses his left hand," she replied.

"Right-handed people usually lick envelope

flaps from left to right.

"Left-handed people usually lick envelope flaps from right to left."

"Excellent, Amber Lee!" Mr. Merlin said. He looked around the room. "I'm glad Amber Lee answered the question."

Noelle blinked. *Why?* she wondered.

"You'll all accomplish more if you work together," Mr. Merlin explained. "That's the way good police detectives do it."

Noelle bowed her head.

She knew Mr. Merlin was talking about her.

She raised her hand.

"Yes, Noelle?" Mr. Merlin said.

"I think we should all work together, too," Noelle said.

Amber Lee gave her a funny look.

But she didn't say anything.

Mr. Merlin smiled. "Well, I'm glad that's settled," he said. "Who knows what we have to do next in order to solve the mystery?"

Todd raised his hand.

"We have to find someone who's left-handed," he said.

"Excellent," Mr. Merlin said.

"That would help you narrow down who might have sent the letter.

"But it's important to remember that the envelope test isn't always accurate.

"Sometimes left-handed people start on the left.

"Sometimes right-handed people start on the right.

"Sometimes people start in the middle and lick to both sides.

"Most of the time, though, left-handed people start on the right, and right-handed people start on the left."

Mr. Merlin looked at the clock on the wall.

"Oh, my!" he said. "We need to do science and spelling before recess!"

So they spent the next hour learning about crocodiles and words that start with *sp*.

Then the bell for recess rang.

"We'll do math after recess," Mr. Merlin said. "Then we'll talk some more about our mystery."

Noelle stood up.

"I can't stand that Amber Lee!" she

whispered to Todd. "She made Mr. Merlin feel sorry for her. Now I think he wants her to solve the mystery!"

Todd grinned. "How can she solve the mystery if we solve it first?"

Chapter Eight

Noelle and Todd hurried outside.

All the other kids in their class were running around the playground, shouting, "Who's left-handed? Who's left-handed?"

"That's not the way to do it," Noelle said.

"Why not?" Todd said.

"Didn't you hear Mr. Merlin?" Noelle said.

"Not all people who are left-handed lick from the right.

"Not all people who are right-handed lick from the left.

"What we need to do is find people who lick from right to left no matter which hand they use!"

"Oh, yeah," Todd said.

Noelle looked over the playground.

She had forgotten that so many kids went to their school.

"We need some *suspects*," she finally said. She looked at Todd. "Do you think it's one of the other boys in our class?"

Todd shook his head.

"No. After Mr. Merlin told us how people licked envelope flaps, I saw Amber Lee ask the boys in the class to show her how they licked theirs.

"They licked them from left to right.

"And they're all right-handed, too.

"I went to sharpen my pencil while we were doing spelling so I could check everyone out.

"They were all using their right hands.

"But Leon needs to practice his cursive writing.

"I could hardly tell what the letters were."

"We have to think of *someone* who might have sent Amber Lee that letter," Noelle said.

"Well, she wasn't in our class last year," Todd said.

"She was in Mrs. Robertson's.

"Maybe it's one of the boys who was in her

class last year but who's in the other third-grade class this year."

"Yes, Todd! That has to be it!" Noelle cried. "I'm sure one of them wrote her that letter."

They ran to the middle of the playground.

They looked around.

Finally, Todd spotted the eight boys in the other third-grade class.

They were playing basketball.

"Let's test them," Noelle said.

She and Todd ran toward the basketball court.

"Hey, you guys. Stop!" Noelle shouted at them. "We have to talk to you!"

The boys stopped their game and stared.

"I'm going to give you a test," Noelle said when she and Todd reached the edge of the basketball court. "I want you to lick the flap of a pretend envelope."

The boys gave her a strange look.

But then they held up their pretend envelopes and licked the flaps.

Noelle watched them carefully.

They all started on the left-hand side.

That meant they hadn't licked the envelope that Amber Lee had received.

The bell rang to end recess.

The boys grumbled about not being able to finish their game.

Noelle and Todd headed back to their side of the building.

They stopped at the water fountain to get a drink.

The second bell rang.

"Oh, no!" Todd cried. "We're late for class!"

They ran down the hall.

They ran into the classroom.

The rest of the class had already started their math problems.

"You're late," Mr. Merlin said. He gave Noelle and Todd a stern look. "If this happens again, I'll have to send you to the office for a tardy slip."

Noelle felt so embarrassed.

She bowed her head.

She walked slowly down the aisle toward her seat.

She passed Leon's desk.

She stopped.

She couldn't believe what she saw.

Leon was doing his math problems with his *left* hand!

Chapter Nine

Noelle waited until they got to the cafeteria to tell Amber Lee what she had discovered.

"Leon sent you that letter," she said.

Amber Lee gasped. *"He did?"*

"Yes, he did," Todd said.

"How did you find out?" Amber Lee asked.

Noelle told Amber Lee what she had seen.

"I think he's really left-handed," she said. "I think he really licks envelope flaps from right to left, too."

"But I tested him!" Amber Lee said. "He licks envelopes from left to right."

"I think he *pretended* to lick envelope flaps from left to right," Todd said. "I think he *pretended* to be right-handed."

Amber Lee sighed. "Well, I can certainly

understand how someone like Leon would look up to me," she said.

Noelle looked around the cafeteria.

She saw Leon sitting at a table on the other side of the room.

But he wasn't eating.

He was staring at them.

Noelle, Todd, and Amber Lee stared back for several minutes.

Finally, Leon looked away.

He stood up.

He picked up his tray.

He put it on the conveyer belt.

Then he walked slowly by their table.

"You'll never prove it," he whispered.

Noelle and Todd looked at each other and grinned.

Amber Lee looked irritated.

During afternoon recess, Noelle and Todd cornered Leon on the playground.

They gave him their evidence.

Leon sighed.

"I thought I fooled you when I licked from

left to right," he said. "I normally lick from right to left."

"You fooled Amber Lee," Todd said.

Leon grinned.

"Did I also fool you when I wrote with my right hand?" he asked.

Todd nodded. "I just thought you couldn't write very well."

"Are you going to tell on me?" Leon said. "The other guys will all make fun of me if you do."

Noelle looked at Todd.

"What do you think we should do?" she asked.

Todd thought for a minute.

"We have to tell Mr. Merlin something," he finally said. "He has to know that we solved the mystery."

So Leon agreed to let them tell Mr. Merlin.

After school, the three of them stayed until everyone else was gone.

Mr. Merlin grinned when he heard what had happened.

"You let down your guard, Leon," he said.

"When you did your math, you weren't

thinking about which hand to write with, so you did what you *normally* do.

"You *normally* use your left hand.

"That's how a lot of criminals get caught.

"They let down their guard."

"You mean I'm a criminal?" Leon asked.

"No. No. Of course not," Mr. Merlin said. "I was just talking about *normal behavior.*"

Leon looked at Noelle and Todd.

"Don't forget," he said. "You promised you wouldn't tell anyone else."

Noelle and Todd looked at Mr. Merlin.

"The rest of the class will want to know the solution to the mystery, Leon," Mr. Merlin said. "We'll have to tell them something. Let me think about it overnight."

The next morning, Mr. Merlin said, "Noelle and Todd have solved Amber Lee's mystery."

"Who sent her the letter?" Misty asked.

All of a sudden, Leon jumped up.

"I did!" he shouted.

The class gasped.

"I wasn't going to tell, because I was too

embarrassed," Leon continued. "But now I'm really excited about how the mystery was solved."

He walked to the front of the room.

"I talked to Mr. Merlin last night. He said our class can solve all kinds of mysteries like this. That's what I want to do."

"Us, too," several other kids said.

"Then that's what we'll do," Mr. Merlin said.

"There are lots of mysteries in our town that need to be solved.

"We'll solve them.

"We'll be the Third-Grade Detectives."

The class cheered.

"Of course, sometimes there are easier ways to solve mysteries like ours," Mr. Merlin said.

"We'll take a field trip tomorrow to the police laboratory to see how Dr. Smiley would have done it."

This was going to be the best third-grade class ever! Noelle thought.

She could hardly wait for tomorrow to come.

Chapter Ten

The next morning, Noelle and Todd got to school early.

A big yellow school bus was parked in front of the building.

Mr. Merlin said Amber Lee could get on first because it was her mystery that had started everything.

Amber Lee climbed up the steps.

She was wearing dark glasses.

When she reached the top step, she turned and waved to the rest of the class.

"Who does she think she is?" Noelle whispered to Todd. "A famous movie star?"

"Hurry up, Amber Lee!" Misty shouted.

Amber Lee gave her a dirty look.

The rest of the class climbed aboard.

Noelle and Todd sat down behind the bus driver.

The bus driver drove downtown.

He stopped the bus in front of a big building.

Noelle saw a sign.

It said, POLICE LABORATORY.

Mr. Merlin stood up. "Remember. We all need to stay together."

A man gave everyone a badge to wear.

The badges said, VISITOR.

Mr. Merlin led the class down a wide hallway.

He seemed to know all the policemen and policewomen in the building.

Finally, the class came to a really big room.

Dr. Smiley was waiting for them.

She was wearing a long white coat.

Noelle thought she looked like a doctor.

"Welcome to the Police Laboratory," Dr. Smiley said.

She pointed to all of the equipment in the room.

"These machines help me solve crimes.

"Mr. Merlin told me how Noelle and Todd solved the mystery of who sent Amber Lee the letter.

"He said it was someone in your class, but he didn't tell me who it was.

"I'm going to show you the way I'd solve the mystery.

"First, I'll start with the evidence.

"That's the flap of Amber Lee's envelope.

"Then I'll use one of these machines to analyze the saliva on it.

"It'll tell me about the DNA.

"Those letters stand for 'deoxyribonucleic acid.'

"It's sort of like building blocks for your body.

"Only one person in the whole world will have the same DNA as what the machine tells me."

"Next, I'll collect saliva samples from each of the suspects.

"That means everyone in the class."

Dr. Smiley gave each person a cotton swab to spit on.

She put each cotton swab inside a glass tube.

She wrote each person's name on the outside of his or her glass tube.

"You misspelled my name," Noelle whispered to Dr. Smiley.

"I'm sorry," Dr. Smiley whispered back.

She scratched out what she had written.

She wrote out "Noelle" correctly.

"Now, I'll use the machine to analyze each saliva sample," Dr. Smiley said.

"In two weeks, I'll tell you who sent the letter to Amber Lee."

Two weeks! Noelle thought.

She was disappointed.

She had hoped they'd find out right away.

Of course, she already knew.

And it hadn't taken her and Todd two weeks to find out, either.

Dr. Smiley took them on a tour of the rest of the laboratory.

She told them about fingerprints.

She told them about hairs and fibers.

She told them about blood.

She told them about fires and burns.

She told them about poisons.

She told them about guns and bullets.

She told them all about how police use science to solve crimes.

Noelle was very impressed.

She made sure she remembered everything.

✉   ✉   ✉

Two weeks later, Dr. Smiley came to their classroom.

"We have a match!" she said.

She held up a cotton swab.

"The DNA of this saliva matches the DNA of the saliva on Amber Lee's envelope flap."

She looked down at the name on the glass tube.

"Leon Dennis!" she said.

The class applauded.

Noelle looked at Leon.

He looked embarrassed.

She remembered how he had tried to fool them by licking the envelope from left to right.

She remembered how he had tried to fool them by writing with his right hand.

He couldn't fool the DNA test, though.

"I have some good news, class," Mr. Merlin said. "Dr. Smiley enjoyed helping us solve Amber Lee's mystery. She'd like us to help her out the next time she has a mystery to solve."

The class let out a cheer.

Can You Break the Code?

Here's a secret message using the stacking code Mr. Merlin explains to the Third-Grade Detectives in chapter two of the book you've just read. But the stacks are in the wrong order! Can you rearrange the stacks and read the message?

```
P  S  A
Y  X  M
A  I  A
```

Oh, no! Here's ANOTHER message with the stacks in the wrong order. Can you figure this one out?

```
O  N  I  G  H
N  E  V  E  S
C  T  X  E  A
L  O  M  E  T
C  K  A  B  C
O  E  M  T  R
```

ANSWERS

The correct order for the first coded message is:

```
A I A
Y X M
P S A
```

Starting with X as the center of the clock, "I" is at noon, so the message is "I AM A SPY" (The "A" on the first line completes the square).

The correct order for the first coded message is:

```
C K A B C
O N I G H
L O M E T
C T X E A
O E M T T
N E V E S
```

Again, starting with X as the center of the clock, the "M" above X is at noon. Moving in a clockwise spiral, the message is "MEET ME TONIGHT AT SEVEN O' CLOCK" (the ABC on the first line completes the square).

Now that you're an expert decoder, have fun making up your own secret messages.

To read the
Third-Grade Detectives'
next adventure,
FLIP THE BOOK.

THIRD–GRADE DETECTIVES #1

The Clue of the
Left–Handed Envelope

THIRD–GRADE DETECTIVES #2

The Puzzle of the
Pretty Pink Handkerchief

George E. Stanley

illustrated by
Salvatore Murdocca

Aladdin Paperbacks
New York London Toronto Sydney

THIRD-GRADE DETECTIVES #2

The Puzzle of the
Pretty Pink Handkerchief

Chapter One

Todd Sloan's mother was in his room talking to him.

But Todd couldn't hear a word she was saying.

His ears were all stopped up.

It had started the night before.

His ears had suddenly closed up.

Then they popped open.

Then they closed up again.

Then they popped open again.

It was driving him crazy.

He had hardly slept at all last night.

"What? What? What?" Todd kept shouting to his mother. "I can't hear you!"

His mother stopped talking.

She gave him a tired look.

Suddenly, Todd's ears popped open.

"Ouch!" he cried.

It really hurt when that happened.

"You can't hear your teacher if your ears are all stopped up, Todd," his mother said. "I'm going to take you to the doctor this morning. He can clean them out."

"But they're not stopped up now, Mom. Honest," Todd said. "Anyway, I can't miss school today."

"Why not?" his mother asked.

"Mr. Merlin said he'd give us a new mystery to solve. What if he does it while I'm at the doctor's office?" Todd looked at her. "I promise! My ears will stay open now."

His mother shook her head in dismay. "I can't believe this. Ever since you started Mr. Merlin's class, you don't want to miss school. Well, finish getting dressed. I'll be back in a minute."

Todd's mother was right.

Mr. Merlin's third-grade class was special.

They were known as the Third-Grade Detectives.

They solved all kinds of mysteries.

It had all started because of Leon Dennis, too!

At the beginning of school, he had sent an unsigned letter to Amber Lee Johnson.

He had written her that she was the smartest girl in the world.

He hadn't thought anybody would know he had done it.

But Mr. Merlin had shown the class how to find out who it was.

Todd and Noelle Trocoderro had solved the mystery.

It was because of Leon's spit.

Mr. Merlin was really impressed by what Todd and Noelle and the rest of the class had done, too.

He'd said they were good enough to help the police solve crimes.

Suddenly, Todd's ears closed up again.

All he could hear was a ringing noise.

He knew he couldn't tell his mother, though.

She would take him to the doctor for sure.

Well, he'd just pretend that he could understand everything his mother said.

All of a sudden, Todd's right ear started to itch.

Todd wished he could crawl inside it and scratch all over.

He tried to ignore the itching.

But it wouldn't stop.

Todd rubbed his ear hard.

But that didn't seem to work, either.

So he took a tissue out of his pocket.

He stuck it just inside his ear.

He removed some earwax.

Finally, his right ear stopped itching.

But both ears were still closed up.

He couldn't hear anything for the ringing noise.

Todd tossed the tissue into the wastebasket.

Why did my ears have to be stopped up now? he wondered.

If he couldn't hear Mr. Merlin, he couldn't hear about the new mystery.

If he couldn't hear about the new mystery, he couldn't solve it.

Todd sighed.

He wished he knew how to read lips.

He had seen people on television do it.

They didn't have to hear people to know what they were saying.

Todd looked up.

His mother was standing at his door.

Her mouth was moving up and down.

Todd knew she was talking.

He watched her lips.

Suddenly, he knew what she was saying!

Your grandmother will take you to the doctor's after school.

Todd couldn't believe it.

He had actually read his mother's lips!

"Okay!" he said.

He grabbed his backpack.

Now it didn't matter if his ears were still stopped up.

He'd be able to read Mr. Merlin's lips.

He'd be able to solve the new mystery.

Chapter Two

Mr. Merlin was standing in front of the class.

His mouth was moving up and down.

But Todd's ears were still stopped up.

He couldn't hear anything Mr. Merlin was saying.

So he was trying to read Mr. Merlin's lips.

He wasn't having much luck.

Todd just hoped he could recognize the word "mystery" if Mr. Merlin said it.

Suddenly, his ears popped open.

"Ouch!" Todd cried.

Mr. Merlin stopped.

"Did somebody poke you, Todd?" he asked.

"No, sir," Todd replied. "My ears just popped open."

"Oh. Okay," Mr. Merlin said. "A lot of people in

school are having ear problems. There's so much pollen in the air."

Now Todd's left ear started to itch.

He thought he could feel something moving around inside it.

He took out a tissue.

He stuck it just inside his ear.

He removed some more earwax.

"Mr. Merlin!" Amber Lee cried. "Todd's sticking something inside his ear!"

Everyone in the class turned to look.

Todd was still holding the tissue in his hand.

"What are you doing now, Todd?" Mr. Merlin asked.

"I'm getting the earwax out of my ear," Todd said. He looked at Mr. Merlin. "Why do I have so much of it?"

"Everyone has earwax," Mr. Merlin said. "But some people have more if they're having problems with their ears."

"Why do we need earwax, anyway?" Noelle said. "It's so gross!"

"Well, earwax keeps the eardrums soft. If the eardrums weren't soft, we couldn't hear very well," Mr. Merlin said. "Earwax also protects our ears. It keeps out dust and dirt and flying insects."

"I'm glad I have earwax," Amber Lee said. "I don't want anything flying around inside my head."

"Why not?" Leon said. "There's plenty of empty space!"

The class laughed.

Todd wondered what an insect would see if it ever got inside Amber Lee's head.

Suddenly, Todd's ears closed up again.

Oh, no! he thought. Now he couldn't take his eyes off of Mr. Merlin's lips!

But Mr. Merlin turned his back to the class.

He started writing spelling words on the board.

Maybe my ears will open up again before we start talking about the new mystery, Todd thought.

What if they didn't, though?

He'd have to be ready to read Mr. Merlin's lips.

But he needed to practice first.

He looked around the room.

He saw Amber Lee talking to Leon.

He watched Amber Lee's lips carefully.

He was sure she had said *police.*

He was sure she had said *principal,* too.

What is Amber Lee talking about? he wondered.

Had the police arrested their principal?

That would be awful.

He really liked Mrs. Jenkins.

His ears popped open.

"Ouch!" he cried.

Mr. Merlin didn't say anything this time.

He kept writing on the chalkboard.

"Did the police arrest Mrs. Jenkins?" Todd whispered to Noelle.

Across the aisle, Misty Goforth gasped. "Mr. Merlin! Mr. Merlin!" she cried. "Why did the police arrest Mrs. Jenkins?"

Mr. Merlin turned around. "What are you talking about, Misty?"

Misty pointed to Todd. "That's what he said."

Todd looked over at Amber Lee. "That's what Amber Lee told Leon."

"I did not!" Amber Lee said.

"Yes, you did!" Todd insisted. "I read your lips."

"Oh!" Amber Lee cried. She looked at Mr. Merlin. "Make him stop, Mr. Merlin! I don't want Todd reading my lips."

"Why are you trying to read people's lips, Todd?" Mr. Merlin asked.

"I only do it when my ears are stopped up," Todd said.

Mr. Merlin smiled. "Well, some people can read lips very well, Todd," he said. "But if you're not trained to do it, you can make mistakes."

"I didn't say the police arrested Mrs. Jenkins," Amber Lee said. "I said the police were in the principal's office this morning."

Mr. Merlin looked surprised.

"They were looking for Johnny Fowler," Leon said. "He played hooky from school again today."

Todd knew Johnny Fowler.

He was in the other third-grade class.

His father owned a bakery.

He made the best doughnuts in town.

Johnny helped him.

Todd had heard that Johnny played hooky a lot.

He wondered where Johnny was when he wasn't in school.

He thought about it for a minute.

If the police didn't know where Johnny was, maybe Mr. Merlin's Third-Grade Detectives could help them.

Todd was sure they could solve this mystery.

Chapter Three

Todd and Noelle were walking home from school.

They lived across the street from each other.

Todd's ears finally stayed open most of the day. He was glad.

Now he didn't have to read anyone else's lips. It was too easy to get into trouble doing that.

And now he didn't have to go to the doctor, either.

His mother had called him at school. His appointment had been cancelled. The doctor had gone home sick.

Todd wasn't glad the doctor was sick. But he was glad he didn't have to have his ears cleaned out today.

"I wonder if the police would let our class find out where Johnny goes when he plays hooky?" Noelle said. "That way they could work on other cases."

"They might. They already know how good we are at solving mysteries," Todd said. "Let's talk to Mr. Merlin about it tomorrow."

Suddenly, Todd's left ear started to itch again.

He could feel something else moving around inside it.

He pulled a tissue out of his pocket.

"You're not going to do that again, are you?" Noelle said.

"You're supposed to clean out your ears, Noelle," Todd said. "Haven't your parents taught you anything?"

Noelle put her hands on her hips. "Yes, they have!" she said. "They taught me that you're not supposed to clean out your ears in front of people!"

Todd grinned.

He looked right at Noelle.

He stuck the tissue inside his ear.

He pulled out some earwax.

"You are so gross!" Noelle said.

Todd started waving the tissue back and forth in front of her,

"Stop that!" Noelle cried.

Todd thrust the tissue at her.

"You'd better stop that," Noelle said. "I'm going to tell your grandmother if you don't."

They had reached Todd's house.

"I'm hungry," Todd said. "Do you want something to eat?"

"Sure," Noelle said.

Todd opened the side gate.

They headed for his back porch.

Todd's grandmother opened the door for them.

During the morning, she was a teacher's aide in the other third-grade class at his school.

Then she came to Todd's house right before Todd got home.

She stayed there until his parents came home from work.

"We're hungry, Grandma," Todd said. "Did you bake me some cookies last night?"

"Don't I always?" his grandmother said.

Todd grinned.

Noelle called her mother to tell her where she was.

Todd's grandmother poured two glasses of

milk and put the cookie platter in the center of the table.

"Can we eat in your tree house?" Noelle whispered.

"That's a great idea," Todd said. "I haven't been up there since last summer."

His grandmother put their milk in plastic cups.

She put their cookies in a plastic bag.

Then Todd and Noelle headed out the back door to the tree house.

Todd held the milk and cookies with one hand.

He used his other hand to climb up the rope ladder.

Noelle was right behind him.

When they were both inside the tree house, Todd said, "Where'd that come from?" He picked up a pink handkerchief.

"You probably left it here last summer," Noelle said.

"I don't use pink handkerchiefs, Noelle," Todd said. "Somebody else has been up here."

He held up the pink handkerchief to the light.

"Well, it's obviously been here for ages," Noelle said. "It's filthy."

17

"It looks like it has earwax on it," Todd said.

Noelle looked closely. "Hey! Maybe that'll tell us whose handkerchief it is."

"That's no clue. All earwax looks the same," Todd said. He pointed to a corner of the pink handkerchief. "Here's the clue. 'JPJ.' That's someone's initials."

"Who's JPJ?" Noelle asked.

"That's the mystery we have to solve," Todd said.

Todd and Noelle finished their milk and cookies.

Then Noelle went home.

Todd went to his room.

He put the pink handkerchief inside a plastic bag and laid it on top of his dresser.

He'd take it to school tomorrow.

He'd show it to Mr. Merlin.

The Third-Grade Detectives now had a new mystery to solve.

Who left the pink handkerchief in Todd's tree house?

Chapter Four

The next morning, Todd gave Mr. Merlin the plastic bag with the pink handkerchief in it.

"What's this?" Mr. Merlin asked.

"It's a new mystery," Todd said. "Someone has been in my tree house. I want to find out who."

Mr. Merlin opened the plastic bag.

He picked up a pencil.

He lifted out the pink handkerchief.

"It has some initials on it," Todd said. "If we can find the person whose name starts with those letters, then we can solve the mystery."

"It's also dirty," Mr. Merlin said.

"That's just earwax. It won't help us solve the mystery," Todd said. "Everyone has earwax."

The bell rang.

Everyone took their seats.

"Todd has a new mystery for us to solve," Mr. Merlin announced. "I'll let him tell you about it."

Todd came to the front of the room.

"Noelle and I found a pink handkerchief in my tree house," he said.

"The pink handkerchief has the initials JPJ on it.

"I want to find out who JPJ is."

"Only kids play in tree houses," Amber Lee said. "So I think it's someone who goes to our school."

"That certainly makes sense," Mr. Merlin said.

"It has to be a girl, too," Leon said.

"Why?" Mr. Merlin asked.

"Only a girl would use a pink handkerchief," Leon said.

Most of the class agreed.

"Okay. We need to find a *girl* at our school who has the initials JPJ," Todd said. "Then we'll know who's been in my tree house without my permission."

"I'm going to give you a secret code clue," Mr. Merlin said.

21

Mr. Merlin used to be a spy.

Todd knew Mr. Merlin liked to give them secret code clues to help them solve a mystery.

He said it made them think better.

Mr. Merlin turned around.

He started writing on the chalkboard.

He wrote:

20–8–5   3–12–21–5   9–19
9–14–19–9–4–5   23–8–1–20   9–19
9–14–19–9–4–5   20–8–5   5–1–18

Numbers! Todd thought. He'd never figure out that secret code clue.

But he didn't need a secret code clue, anyway.

All he had to do was be the first one to find a girl with the initials JPJ.

When the recess bell rang, Todd and Noelle hurried out the door.

"There's no girl in our class whose initials are JPJ," Noelle said. "I wonder which class she's in."

"That's what we have to find out," Todd said. "That's why we're detectives."

They started across the playground.

The other members of their class were looking for JPJ, too.

They were asking all the kids their names.

When the kids asked them why they wanted to know, they said they were just playing a game.

"Look!" Noelle said.

She pointed to a far corner of the playground.

Amber Lee was talking to a redheaded girl.

"Come on," Todd said. "We can't let her be the first one to solve my mystery!"

They ran across the playground.

"I found her. Jana Pauline Jones," Amber Lee said. "She's in the other third grade class."

"Hi," Jana said to Todd and Noelle.

Todd knew right away that something was wrong.

Both Amber Lee and Jana Pauline sounded sad.

"What's wrong?" Todd asked.

"I used to have a pink handkerchief. It had my initials on it," said Jana Pauline. "My grandmother gave it to me."

"What happened to it?" Noelle asked.

"I left it in my desk," Jana said. She sniffed. "Somebody stole it."

"Did you use it to clean out your ears?" Todd asked.

Jana gasped.

"I'd never do anything like that with my pretty handkerchiefs!" she said.

Amber Lee stamped her foot.

"It's not fair!" she said. "I thought we had this case solved."

Todd couldn't believe it.

He'd never thought of that.

He now knew who owned the handkerchief.

But it wasn't the same person who had left it in his tree house.

The bell to end recess rang.

Todd and Noelle walked slowly back to their classroom.

When everyone was seated, Mr. Merlin said, "Any luck?"

Todd told him what had happened.

"Well, has anyone solved the secret code clue yet?" Mr. Merlin asked.

No one had.

"Then I'll give you some rules," Mr. Merlin said.

Todd knew he had to listen carefully.

If he wanted to solve this mystery, he'd have to use the secret code clue after all.

"There are twenty–six letters in the alphabet," Mr. Merlin said. "Read them from left to right."

Chapter Five

Todd was disappointed.

He had hoped Mr. Merlin would give them a better clue.

Everyone knew there were twenty–six letters in the alphabet.

Everyone knew you read the letters from left to right, too.

But how will that help me solve the secret code clue? Todd wondered.

He looked over at Amber Lee.

She wasn't working on the secret code clue.

She was showing Leon a picture of Dr. Smiley.

Dr. Smiley was Mr. Merlin's friend.

She was a police scientist.

She used science to solve crimes.

Amber Lee was always telling people that she was going to be just like Dr. Smiley when she grew up.

Todd didn't think Amber Lee could ever be as good as Dr. Smiley.

He looked at the secret code clue again.

20–8–5   3–12–21–5   9–19
9–14–19–9–4–5   23–8–1–20   9–19
9–14–19–9–4–5   20–8–5   5–1–18

Was Mr. Merlin talking about which *number* each letter was?

Todd got out a sheet of notebook paper.

He wrote the numbers 1 through 26 in a column down the side.

Then, next to each number, he wrote a letter of the alphabet.

He started with *A* for 1.

He ended with *Z* for 26.

The first word of the secret code clue was 20–8–5.

Todd looked at the numbers with the alphabet on his piece of paper.

20 was *t*. 8 was *h*. 5 was *e*.

The!

Yes! he thought.

Now he knew how to solve it!

He matched the rest of the numbers of the secret code clue with the numbers on his piece of paper.

The secret code clue was: *The clue is inside what is inside the ear.*

What in the world does that mean? he wondered.

Suddenly, Todd's left ear started to itch again.

His ears weren't opening and closing anymore.

But he was still getting a lot of earwax out of them.

Todd was glad Mr. Merlin had told the class that earwax was a normal thing.

He didn't want people to think he was the only one who had a lot of it.

He took a tissue out of his pocket.

He stuck it just inside his ear.

He removed some of the earwax.

He looked at it for several seconds.

That's it! he thought.

Todd started waving his hand in the air.

"Mr. Merlin! Mr. Merlin!" he said. "I know what the secret code clue is!"

There was a lot of groaning in the room.

Several people said they had almost solved it, too.

"What does it say, Todd?" Mr. Merlin asked.

"The clue is inside what is inside the ear," Todd said.

"That's right," Mr. Merlin said. "Do you know what it means?"

Todd nodded.

He showed the class his tissue.

"This!" he said.

"Earwax can't be a clue," Amber Lee said. "Everybody has earwax."

"The clue is not the earwax," Todd said. "The clue is what's trapped *inside* the earwax!"

"Excellent!" Mr. Merlin said.

Just then, the lunch bell rang.

Chapter Six

It took Todd and Noelle several minutes to get their food trays.

The cooks had to make some more macaroni and cheese.

Now there were only two seats left at the tables where Mr. Merlin's class sat.

And they were across from Amber Lee and Leon.

"Why do we need to know what's inside *your* earwax?" Amber Lee demanded when Todd sat down in front of her. "That's not going to help us solve the mystery."

"It's not *my* earwax," Todd said. "It's the earwax on the pink handkerchief."

"We need to find out what's trapped inside it," Noelle said. "It may be something that will

tell us who was in Todd's tree house."

"Oh!" Amber Lee said. "I wish I had thought of that."

"How can we find out?" Leon asked.

Todd sighed. "I don't know," he said.

"I know!" Amber Lee said.

Todd looked at her. "How?"

"Dr. Smiley!"

"Do you think Mr. Merlin would take us back to the Police Laboratory?" Todd said.

"He won't have to do that. I'm having a meeting at Dr. Smiley's house after school today," Amber Lee said. "I can find out then."

Todd and Noelle gave her a puzzled look.

"I didn't know that," Todd said.

"Why didn't somebody tell us?" Noelle said.

"You're not invited," Amber Lee said.

"It's just for me.

"I'm going to talk to Dr. Smiley about starting a fan club.

"I want to be just like her when I grow up."

"That's not fair!" Noelle said.

"We like Dr. Smiley, too," Todd said.

"That doesn't make any difference," Amber

Lee said. "You can start your own fan club."

"Does Mr. Merlin know you're doing this?" Todd asked.

Amber Lee didn't say anything.

"I bet he doesn't," Noelle said. "He won't like it when he finds out."

Amber Lee looked at Leon.

"He won't mind," Leon said hurriedly.

"Yes, he will," Todd said. "He wants us all to cooperate."

"And you're not cooperating, Amber Lee," Noelle said.

"Okay! Okay!" Amber Lee said. "You can be members of the Dr. Smiley Fan Club."

Yes! Todd thought.

He wanted to be like Dr. Smiley when he grew up, too.

❋ ❋ ❋

When they got back to their classroom, Amber Lee said, "Mr. Merlin, may I make an announcement?"

"Yes, you may," Mr. Merlin said.

Amber Lee stood up.

"I'm starting a Dr. Smiley Fan Club," she said.

"I'm having the first meeting after school today.

"It'll be at Dr. Smiley's house.

"She's going to show me her home laboratory.

"She works there sometimes.

"I'm going to ask Dr. Smiley to help me find out what's trapped inside the earwax on Todd's pink handkerchief."

Oh, brother! Todd thought.

Amber Lee looked over at Mr. Merlin.

"I always try very hard to cooperate," she continued, "so I'll let anyone who wants to join my club."

"That is very nice of you, Amber Lee," Mr. Merlin said. He turned to the rest of the class. "You're all doing a great job trying to solve this mystery. Keep up the good work."

Noelle looked at Todd and rolled her eyes.

For the rest of the day, they did schoolwork.

Mr. Merlin always made it interesting, but the day still seemed to drag by.

Todd could hardly wait until the last bell.

He wanted to get to Dr. Smiley's house.

He wanted to find out what was trapped inside the earwax on the pink handkerchief.

Chapter Seven

When the last bell rang, Todd hurried to the principal's office.

He telephoned his mother at work.

When she answered, he said, "We're going to Dr. Smiley's house, Mom.

"Mr. Merlin is walking there with us.

"We're having a meeting of the Dr. Smiley Fan Club.

"We're going to solve a mystery, too."

"Okay. Just call me when the meeting's over. I'll come pick you up," his mother said. "I'll also let your grandmother know that you won't be home."

"Thanks, Mom," Todd said.

He hurried out of the principal's office.

The rest of the class was waiting for him in the parking lot.

Mr. Merlin handed Todd the plastic bag with the pink handkerchief.

"You may give this to Dr. Smiley when we get to her house," he said.

Todd felt really important now.

Dr. Smiley lived three blocks from the school.

When they got there, Dr. Smiley was waiting for them on her front porch.

She was smiling.

Todd wondered what she would be doing if her name were Dr. Frowny.

The class followed Dr. Smiley into her house.

She led them to the kitchen.

"I thought we'd have a snack before we start the meeting," she said.

Todd saw a huge platter of cookies in the center of a table.

There was also a stack of plastic cups and three cartons of milk on the cabinet.

Dr. Smiley and Mr. Merlin poured the milk.

The class helped themselves to cookies.

They were store–bought.

Todd didn't think they were as good as his grandmother's.

But he still ate six of them.

Finally, everyone was full.

There weren't very many cookies left on the huge platter.

Dr. Smiley took everyone downstairs to the basement.

This was where she had her home laboratory.

"When do you work here?" Noelle asked.

"Sometimes I wake up in the middle of the night and think I have the answer to a problem at work," Dr. Smiley said. "I come down here then.

"I also use it if I'm tired of being in the office and want to get away.

"Sometimes, I use it for my personal research."

Amber Lee looked at Dr. Smiley. "Shall I call the meeting to order now?" she asked.

Dr. Smiley smiled. "That's fine with me, Amber Lee. Actually, I've never had a fan club before. I don't know exactly what we're supposed to do."

"I know," Amber Lee said. "I've been a member of a lot of fan clubs."

Everyone sat down on the floor.

Amber Lee stood next to a table.

"I'm calling this meeting to order," Amber Lee said. "Everyone but me has to quit talking."

She sure is bossy, Todd thought.

Amber Lee pulled a piece of paper out of her pocket.

"The first thing we need to do is elect officers," Amber Lee said. "I've come up with a slate of candidates."

Todd had no idea what Amber Lee was talking about.

He thought all they'd do was talk about the earwax on the pink handkerchief.

Amber Lee started reading.

"Amber Lee Johnson for president, vice president, secretary, and treasurer."

Amber Lee looked up.

"Do I hear a second?"

"Second!" Leon said.

"All in favor say 'Aye,'" Amber Lee said.

Amber Lee and Leon said, "Aye!"

The rest of the class just looked at each other.

"Now, as your president, vice president,

secretary, and treasurer," Amber Lee began, "the first thing I'd like to do is—"

Todd stood up. "How'd you get to be all those people, Amber Lee?"

Amber Lee gave him a hard look. "You're out of order, Todd Sloan. Sit down."

"No!" Todd said.

Mr. Merlin stood up.

"Maybe we should postpone the organization of the Dr. Smiley Fan Club until another time," he said.

"That might be a good idea," Dr. Smiley said. "I think we need to discuss this further."

Todd held up the plastic bag.

"Does that mean we can't find out what's trapped inside the earwax on the pink handkerchief?"

"No, I think that's one thing we can do today," Dr. Smiley said.

She took the plastic bag from Todd.

This is more like it, Todd thought.

In just a few minutes, he'd know who had been in his tree house without his permission.

Chapter Eight

"I'm glad you put the handkerchief in a plastic bag, Todd. That was the right thing to do," Dr. Smiley said. "You should always protect your evidence."

Todd smiled.

He was glad Dr. Smiley thought he was a good detective.

Dr. Smiley used some tweezers to lift the handkerchief out of the plastic bag.

Next, she carefully laid the handkerchief on a glass counter.

"Let's review what we know about this evidence," Dr. Smiley began.

"We know that two weeks ago someone stole this pink handkerchief out of Jana Pauline Jones's desk.

"We know that somehow it got earwax on it."

"Jana Pauline Jones didn't do it," Amber Lee said. She looked over at Todd. "She said she would never clean out her ears with one of her pretty handkerchiefs."

Dr. Smiley smiled.

The she looked closely at the earwax.

She touched it with a small knife.

"This earwax is still soft," she said.

"I'm sure it's not older than two weeks.

"Here's what I think happened.

"Whoever stole the pink handkerchief used it to clean out his or her ears.

"He or she probably did it in Todd's tree house.

"Since the pink handkerchief was now dirty, he or she must have decided to leave it there.

"He or she didn't realize it was evidence.

"This happens to a lot of criminals.

"They'll leave things at the scene of a crime that will help the police capture them."

Todd knew Dr. Smiley was talking about Leon.

Leon hadn't realized he was leaving behind his spit when he had sent Amber Lee a secret letter.

"Okay, detectives. Gather around the table," Dr. Smiley said. "Now we'll examine the earwax itself."

Everyone got as close to the table as possible.

"We'll take some of the earwax and put it on a microscope slide," Dr. Smiley continued.

She used a small knife to scrape off some of the earwax from the pink handkerchief.

She spread it in the center of the glass slide.

"That's just like spreading peanut butter on bread," Leon said.

"Oh, yuck!" Noelle said.

She moved away from Leon.

Next, Dr. Smiley put another glass slide on top of the first glass slide.

She held it up to the light.

"This should do nicely," she said.

She put the slide under the lens of the micro-scope.

She looked into the eyepiece.

Todd watched as she turned some knobs.

"This is interesting," Dr. Smiley said. "This is *very* interesting."

"What do you see?" Todd asked excitedly.

He moved closer to the microscope.

After all, he had found the pink handkerchief.

He should be the first one to find out what was trapped inside the earwax.

"Well, I see some things that you'd expect to see in earwax," Dr. Smiley said.

"I see particles of tree pollen.

"That's normal.

"All of the trees are starting to bud."

"How do you know that's what it is?" Noelle asked.

Dr. Smiley smiled. "I studied this in school. You have to remember what all kinds of things look like under the microscope."

Todd thought about that.

From now on, he'd try to remember everything that Mr. Merlin told them in class.

That way, he could do what Dr. Smiley did.

"What else do you see?" Amber Lee asked.

"I see some particles of dirt," Dr. Smiley said. "That's normal, too.

"But I also see something that not everybody has trapped in his or her earwax."

"What?" Todd asked.

"I see particles of flour dust," Dr. Smiley said.

She looked up from the microscope.

"I'm sure this earwax belonged to someone who's done some baking lately," she said.

Baking! Todd thought.

"The only person I know who bakes things is my grandmother," Todd whispered to Noelle.

Noelle gasped.

Did that mean his grandmother had stolen Jana Pauline Jones's handkerchief? Todd wondered.

Did that mean his grandmother had cleaned her ears with it?

Did that mean his grandmother had been up in his tree house?

Chapter Nine

Todd's mother was waiting for him in front of Dr. Smiley's house.

He got into the car.

He didn't say anything.

His mother drove away.

After a few minutes, his mother said, "Why are you so quiet, Todd? Is there anything wrong?"

Todd looked over at her.

"Do you think Grandma could have left that pink handkerchief in my tree house?" he said.

His mother started laughing.

"What in the world gave you that idea, Tood?" she asked.

"Dr. Smiley said whoever used the pink handkerchief to clean out his ears had baked something recently," Todd explained.

His mother looked puzzled.

"How did she know that?" she asked.

So Todd told her about earwax.

He explained how it traps particles from the air.

He explained how that keeps the particles from getting into the ear.

"The earwax on the pink handkerchief had particles of flour dust in it.

"Grandma is the only person I know who uses flour to bake things.

"She's also a teacher's aide in Jana Pauline Jones's class.

"She could have taken the pink handkerchief when Jana wasn't looking.

"Who else could it be?"

"Oh, now I understand why you might think that," his mother said.

"In fact, it shows a lot of thought on your part.

"But your grandmother couldn't have done it, Todd.

"First of all, she'd never take anything that wasn't hers.

"And her arthritis is too bad for her to climb

up that rope to get into your tree house.

"No, it has to be someone else who's been around flour dust.

"There are a lot of people in town who bake things."

They had reached their house.

His mother drove into the garage.

Todd was happy now.

He wanted to solve the mystery.

But he didn't want his grandmother to be the answer.

* * *

It was almost time for the bell to ring when Todd got to school the next day. He hurried into Mr. Merlin's room. He sat down in his desk.

"Grandma didn't do it. She has arthritis," he whispered to Noelle. "She can't climb up into my tree house. Someone else left the pink handkerchief there."

Noelle looked disappointed. "I thought we had solved the mystery," she whispered back.

"I did, too. But I'm glad Grandma didn't do it," Todd whispered. "I didn't want the police to arrest her."

Suddenly, Misty came rushing into the room.

She sat down.

She leaned over to Noelle.

"Guess what?" Misty whispered.

But she whispered so loud that Todd could hear every word.

"What?" Noelle whispered back.

"Johnny Fowler played hooky again today.

"His father was in the principal's office.

"Mrs. Jenkins was talking to him."

"How did you know it was Johnny's father?" Noelle asked.

"We buy our doughnuts from his bakery. I'd recognize him anywhere," Misty said. "He had flour dust all over his clothes."

Of course! Todd thought. *Why didn't I think of that?*

Now he knew who had stolen Jana Pauline Jones's pink handkerchief.

Now he knew who had left it in his tree house.

The only thing he had to do was prove it.

Chapter Ten

Todd looked at the big clock on the wall.

It was almost time for the last bell to ring.

He wanted to be by the door when it did.

He had to get home fast.

He got up from his desk.

He walked to the pencil sharpener.

He pretended to sharpen his pencil.

The bell rang.

Todd hurried out of the classroom.

He ran across the parking lot.

He ran down the sidewalk.

He turned the corner.

Up ahead, he saw Johnny Fowler coming out the side gate of his backyard.

Johnny started walking in the opposite direction.

"Johnny!" Todd shouted. "Wait for me!"

But Johnny kept walking.

"Johnny!" Todd shouted again.

But Johnny didn't stop walking.

He acts like he doesn't hear me, Todd thought.

Finally, Todd reached Johnny.

He touched him on the shoulder.

Johnny whirled around.

"What do you want?" he said.

"I want to talk to you," Todd said.

Johnny gave Todd a funny look. "What? What? I can't hear you!" he said.

His ears are stopped up just like mine were! Todd realized.

Suddenly, Johnny said, "Ouch!"

"What's wrong?" Todd asked.

"Nothing," Johnny said.

But he was rubbing his right ear.

"I know where you are when you're not in school," Todd said.

"Where?" Johnny said.

"You're in my tree house," Todd said.

"I am not," Johnny said.

He took a tissue out of his pocket.

He cleaned his right ear with it.

"I can prove it," Todd said.

"How?" Johnny asked.

"Let me have that tissue," Todd said.

Johnny looked down at the tissue in his hand.

"Why?" he said.

"It's evidence," Todd said.

Johnny thought about it for a minute.

Then he shrugged.

He handed Todd the tissue with his earwax on it.

"Come with me to Dr. Smiley's house," Todd said. "I'll show you how I know it's you."

Todd told his grandmother where they were going.

When they got to Dr. Smiley's house, she was just pulling into her driveway.

Todd introduced her to Johnny.

Then he gave Dr. Smiley the tissue Johnny had used to clean his ear.

"Can you show Johnny what's trapped inside his earwax?" he said.

Dr. Smiley looked at Johnny. "Is this all right with you?" she asked.

Johnny nodded.

Dr. Smiley took them down to her laboratory.

She scraped Johnny's earwax off the tissue.

She put it on a slide.

She looked at it under the microscope.

She turned to Johnny.

"You take a look," she said.

Johnny looked into the microscope.

"What are those funny-looking things I see?" he asked.

"They're particles of pollen, dirt, and flour dust," Dr. Smiley said.

"How did that stuff get into my earwax?" Johnny asked.

Todd explained it to him.

"Does that prove I was in Todd's tree house?" Johnny asked.

"No, Johnny," Dr. Smiley said. "It doesn't really prove that you were in the tree house."

Todd looked disappointed. "Why not?" he asked.

"Well, the flour dust in the earwax on the pink handkerchief is the same as the flour dust in the earwax on the tissue," Dr. Smiley explained.

"And I think the earwax on the pink handkerchief and the earwax on this tissue belong to the same person.

"But someone else besides Johnny could have put the pink handkerchief in the tree house.

"That's what a lawyer would say."

Todd and Dr. Smiley both looked at Johnny.

"I did it," Johnny said. "I left the pink handkerchief in Todd's tree house."

Todd thought Johnny seemed really happy that he'd been caught.

* * *

The next morning at school, there was a meeting in Mrs. Jenkins's office.

Johnny Fowler was there.

So was his father.

So were Todd and Mr. Merlin.

Johnny wanted them to be there.

He told everyone what his problem was.

He didn't want to work so much at the bakery.

He wanted to do more things at school.

Johnny's father apologized.

He hadn't realized this.

Ever since Johnny's mother had died, Mr. Fowler hadn't done anything but work in the bakery.

He wanted Johnny to be there with him.

He had forgotten that Johnny needed to do other things.

"I want to be like the other kids at school, Dad," he said. He turned to Todd. "I want to do what you do."

Mr. Merlin had a solution.

He had already talked to Mrs. Jenkins about it.

He had already talked to Johnny's teacher, too.

Johnny would move to Mr. Merlin's class.

Johnny thought that was a wonderful idea.

Todd agreed.

"But you have to apologize to Jana Pauline Jones for taking her pink handkerchief," Mrs. Jenkins said.

Johnny looked embarrassed.

But he said, "I will."

Todd looked at him. "Do you like her? Is that

why you took her pink handkerchief?"

Johnny looked surprised. "No. I just needed something to clean my ears. Jana has so many pretty handkerchiefs, I didn't think she'd mind."

Todd laughed.

He was sure Johnny would fit right in with the rest of the Third-Grade Detectives.

Biters Beware!

Police scientists can solve crimes by looking at what's inside your ears. That's what Dr. Smiley did with earwax in the book you've just read. Police scientists can also solve crimes by looking at what's inside your mouth. Here's an experiment you can do at school (or with friends at home) to see how they do it.

1. Get four apples.

2. Choose four classmates and give each of them an apple. It's best to choose four class- mates whose teeth don't look the same.

3. Out of sight of the rest of the class, have each classmate take one bite out of his or her apple.

4. Line up the apples on a table so everyone can see the bite mark in each apple.

5. Can you tell who bit into which apple?

To match up the biters with the apples, all you have to do is ask each biter to open his or her mouth, and compare the person's teeth to the teeth marks on the apple.

Police scientists often solve crimes by com- paring a suspect's teeth with the teeth marks found on discarded food at the scene of a crime. Criminals who rob grocery stores or other places where food is sold will often eat part of a piece of fruit or pastry during a robbery and then leave it at the scene of a crime. Police scientists love to find this kind of evidence!

Want more
Third-Grade Detectives?
Here's an excerpt from the
next book in the series.

THIRD-GRADE DETECTIVES #3

The Mystery of the Hairy Tomatoes

Chapter One

Noelle Trocoderro raised her hand.

"Yes, Noelle?" Mr. Merlin said.

"The police tried to arrest my dog, Rover, last night," Noelle said.

Mr. Merlin looked puzzled. "Why?"

"They said he tore up some of Mrs. Ruston's tomato plants," Noelle said.

"But Rover didn't do it. He had an alibi. He was asleep in my room when it happened."

"Oh, yes, I heard about the tomato plants this morning," Mr. Merlin said. "But I didn't know that Rover was a suspect in the crime."

Noelle nodded.

Then Mr. Merlin told the rest of the class what had happened.

1

Mrs. Ruston was one of the fifth-grade teachers at their school.

She and her husband owned a small farm at the edge of town.

They grew vegetables to sell to the local grocery stores.

They were famous for their tomatoes.

During the night, somebody had torn up several of the tomato plants.

Mrs. Ruston said it looked like a dog had been digging around in them.

"The police are investigating it," Mr. Merlin said. He looked at Noelle. "Why would Mrs. Ruston think that Rover did it?"

"He tore up some of her flowers last month," Noelle said. "She's still mad at him because of that."

Todd Sloan raised his hand.

"Could we help the police solve the mystery, Mr. Merlin?" he asked. "Could we find the dog that did it?"

"That's a good idea, Mr. Merlin," Noelle said. "If we could find the real dog, then Mrs. Ruston would know that Rover didn't do it."

"I'm sure the police would appreciate any help the Third-Grade Detectives could give them," Mr. Merlin said.

Amber Lee raised her hand.

"Yes, Amber Lee?" Mr. Merlin said.

"I bought a pretty greeting card for Preston Edwards," Amber Lee said. "I want everybody to sign it."

"Who's Preston Edwards?" Leon Dennis asked.

"He's that new kid with long, blond hair," Todd said. "He's in the other third-grade class."

"He just moved across the street from me," Amber Lee said.

"And he's really nervous about going to a new school.

"He doesn't know if the kids here will like him.

"So I want to make him feel welcome.

"That's why I bought him this card. It says: 'We're glad you're here.'"

"Amber Lee has a boyfriend!" Leon sang. "Amber Lee has a boyfriend!"

"I do not!" Amber Lee cried.

"That's enough, Leon," Mr. Merlin said.

He turned to Amber Lee.

3

"I think it was nice of you to get Preston a card, Amber Lee," he said. "Yes, you may let everyone sign it."

Amber Lee began passing the card around the room.

Johnny Fowler raised his hand. "How do we start to solve the mystery, Mr. Merlin?" he asked.

Noelle raised her hand.

"I know! I know!" she said.

"Okay, Noelle," Mr. Merlin said. "Tell us."

"We go to Mrs. Ruston's farm," Noelle said.

"That's the scene of the crime.

"We look for evidence there."

"What kind of evidence?" Johnny asked.

Noelle didn't know what kind of evidence they were supposed to look for.

Why did Johnny have to ask her a question she couldn't answer?

Now she wished she hadn't even raised her hand.

She looked over at Mr. Merlin.

"I'm going to give you a secret code clue," Mr. Merlin said. "It'll tell you what kind of evidence to look for."

He turned around.

He started writing on the chalkboard.

He wrote:

OLLP ULI HLNVGSRMT GSZG GSV HFHKVXG OVUG YVSRMW

Noelle knew that Johnny was looking at her.

She knew he expected her to solve the secret code clue so he'd know what evidence to look for.

She could tell he thought she was really smart.

She didn't want to disappoint him.

She looked at the secret code clue again.

Unfortunately, she had no idea what it meant.

And she knew Mr. Merlin wouldn't give them any rules for the secret code until they had tried to solve it without them.

He said that solving secret codes made them think better.

Noelle hoped she could find some evidence before someone else solved the secret code clue.

She didn't want Johnny to think she wasn't the smartest girl in the class after all.